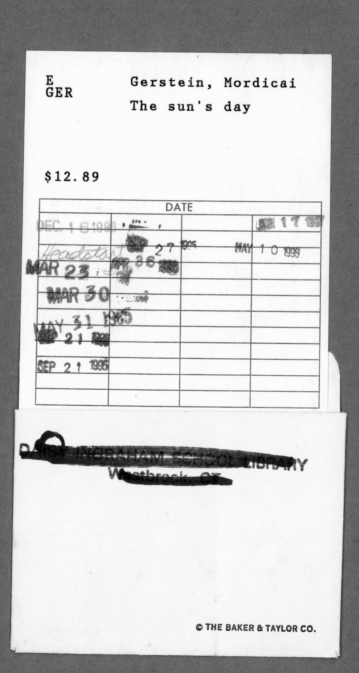

E
GER

Gerstein, Mordicai

The sun's day

$12.89

DATE			
DEC 1 6 1992			JAN 1 7 1997
Headstart 27 1995		MAY 1 0 1996	
MAR 23 86			
MAR 30			
MAY 31 1989			
21 1995			
SEP 2 1 1995			

THE SUN'S DAY

MORDICAI GERSTEIN

HARPER & ROW, PUBLISHERS

For
Risa Faye Amelia Harris-Gerstein

and for
Wallace Stevens, "that brave man"

Library of Congress Cataloging-in-Publication Data
Gerstein, Mordicai.
   The sun's day / Mordicai Gerstein.
      p.   cm.
   Summary: An hour-by-hour description of the activities that take
place as the sun rises, moves through the sky, and finally sets.
   ISBN 0-06-022404-5.   ISBN 0-06-022405-3 (lib. bdg.)
   [1. Sun—Fiction.   2. Day—Fiction.]   I. Title.
PZ7.G325Su 1989   88-24738
[E]—dc19   CIP
                                                                 AC

At 5 o'clock in the morning

the sun comes up and begins the day.

At 6 o'clock in the morning

chirping chicks pop out of eggs.

At 7 o'clock in the morning

babies wake and want breakfast.

At 8 o'clock in the morning

butter melts on warm toast.

At 9 o'clock in the morning

horns honk and bells ring.

At 10 o'clock in the morning

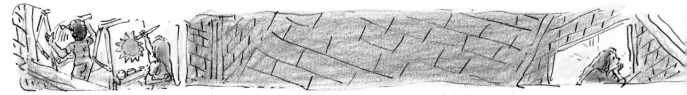

bees buzz and gather honey.

At 11 o'clock in the morning

wheels and gears clank and whirr.

At 12 noon

hungry workers stop for lunch.

At 1 o'clock in the afternoon

cats curl up and nap.

At 2 o'clock in the afternoon

peaches are ripe and ready to pick.

At 3 o'clock in the afternoon

balls go bouncing through the air.

At 4 o'clock in the afternoon

kites flutter down to be taken home.

At 5 o'clock in the afternoon

soup pots are simmering.

At 6 o'clock in the evening

pictures of sunsets are painted.

At 7 o'clock in the evening

babies take baths and say "Good night!"

At 8 o'clock in the evening

the sun goes down and begins the night.